THE GREAT CAKE RACE

Teresa Heapy

ILLUSTRATED BY Erica Salcedo

BLOOMSBURY EDUCATION

LONDON   OXFORD   NEW YORK   NEW DELHI   SYDNEY

BLOOMSBURY EDUCATION
Bloomsbury Publishing Plc
50 Bedford Square, London, WC1B 3DP, UK
29 Earlsfort Terrace, Dublin 2, Ireland

BLOOMSBURY, BLOOMSBURY EDUCATION and the Diana logo are trademarks of
Bloomsbury Publishing Plc

First published in Great Britain in 2022 by Bloomsbury Publishing Plc

A catalogue record for this book is available from the British Library

ISBN: PB: 978-1-8019-9135-3; ePDF: 978-1-8019-9133-9; ePub: 978-1-8019-9134-6

2 4 6 8 10 9 7 5 3 1

Text design by Sarah Malley

Printed and bound by CPI Group (UK) Ltd, Croydon, CR0 4YY

MIX
Paper from
responsible sources
FSC® C171272

To find out more about our authors and books visit www.bloomsbury.com
and sign up for our newsletters

THE GREAT CAKE RACE

CONTENTS

CHAPTER ONE

Jamila read the notice on the park gate with her heart thumping. *I can do that!* She thought. *I know I can do that!*

Jamila was seven years old. She loved

cake. And she was a very good runner.
So this was perfect.

Wasn't it?

The only problem was, Jamila had
never made a cake on her own.

She wasn't going to let that stop her,
though. Jamila didn't let anything stop
her. Whether it was drawing, dancing,
running or reading, Jamila always went
for it. She chose the fastest route, the
brightest colours and the boldest patterns.

"My joyful Jamila," her Nani – her
grandma – had called her, before she'd
died nine months ago.

"Look, Dad – it's a race with cakes!"
said Jamila, jumping up and down.

"Can *I* enter? Can I? Can I?"

"Yeah… why not?" said her dad, ruffling her hair. He took a leaflet from the folder beside the poster. "I've always told you, Jamila. You can do anything."

"ANYTHING!" agreed Farhan, her two-year-old brother, snatching the leaflet and trying to eat it.

THE GREAT CAKE RACE!
★★★ Saturday 3 May, 10 am ★★★
Honeysuckle Community Centre and Park
Make a cake and race it to the finish line
Fastest cake wins!

"What sort of cake do I need to bake?" said Jamila, her feet jigging with excitement.

"Let's see…" Dad gently tugged the half-eaten leaflet away from Farhan and looked at it more closely. "*No help from anyone else… Has to be put in the oven by the judges if contestant under 14 years old…* blah blah blah… *Cake has to be whole when brought over the finishing line…* Good luck with that! Ah yes, here it is. *Cake to be an original creation of your own choice.*"

"An o-ri-gi-what now?" asked Jamila. "What's that? Does it have raisins?"

"Raisins!" said Farhan, nodding excitedly.

"It means it has to come from *your head*," said her dad with a smile. "It has to be full of joyful Jamila!"

Jamila's eyes sparkled. She was going to make a cake like no one had ever seen before. A cake with *everything* in it.

CHAPTER TWO

"Sponge cake," said a voice as Jamila stood there, dreaming about her amazing cake. "No time for fruit cake. Gotta do it in an hour and a half, see – then race it. You gonna enter?" A boy with freckles and long shorts took a leaflet and grinned at Jamila. "You're in Year Three aren't you? I'm Freddie."

"I'm Jamila." Jamila grinned back. Freddie was in Year Five at school, but he was really friendly. In fact, everyone round here was friendly. Jamila and her family had moved to Honeysuckle Estate six months ago, and they'd had a steady stream of welcoming plants, invitations and lasagnes from Lulu and her family (who lived next door), Stuart and Jane (who lived two doors down) and most of the cast of the Community Centre panto, which happened every Christmas.

("Although I can cook," Jamila's dad had said to her mum, privately. "The neighbours do know I can cook, right?") Jamila's mum was a lawyer. Jamila's dad picked her up from school every day, and looked after her and Farhan. Jamila's mum came home at 6 pm every night and they had dinner together.

"You should enter," said Freddie. "It's great fun. Last year, Stuart *nearly* won with this pink, four-layer strawberry sponge. I don't know how he got it over the finishing line in one piece, but he did! I think four layers is the way to go…"

"AND it was delicious," said Lulu, coming up and taking a leaflet. "The best part, pet, is we get to eat a bit of everyone's cake at the end. But you'd better get in quick. Only four contestants, you see. Only four ovens! I'm definitely entering again. You give it a go. You never know, this might be the year that someone else…"

"*Someone else* wins? I don't think so," said a weaselly voice from behind Jamila.

Jamila span round. It was Jasper Dedicoat. He lived six doors down.

He hadn't made them a lasagne.

"Jasper wins every year," said Freddie. He sounded polite, but his face looked like someone had stepped on his toe. Behind them, Dad wrestled with Farhan, who was now jumping up and down demanding a cake *right now*.

"And he deserves every cup he's won,"

said Lulu, suddenly sounding a little *too* cheery.

"Unbroken record," said Jasper, dryly.

"But we welcome new contestants, don't we?" said Lulu.

Jasper eyed Jamila with beetly black eyes. "Always room for new bods. But you won't win, will you?"

"Hang on–" began Freddie.

"UNBROKEN RECORD SINCE RECORDS BEGAN," continued Jasper.

"Well, it only started five years ago…" began Lulu.

"**UNBROKEN RECORD**," repeated Jasper. "And this year… the prize is being presented by TV baker, Bernard Bun."

"*Bernard Bun off 'BAKE ME A CAKE'*?!" said Lulu, clutching her heart. "Oh my goodness! I've got to win!"

"Good luck with that," Jasper sneered, going off with a snide smile. Dad finally emerged from his Farhan-wrestle and looked suspiciously at Jasper's back.

"What's going on?" he said.

"Just Jasper. You take no notice, pet," said Lulu to Jamila.

"Yeah! You go for it, Jamila," said Freddie.

"Goforit!" repeated Farhan, jumping up and down.

There was no question about it now. Jamila, Dad and Farhan raced to the Community Centre to put down Jamila's name.

Then they raced home.

Jamila raced to the oven.

"C'mon, Dad, let's start baking!"

CHAPTER THREE

It turned out that Jamila's dad, although he was a great cook, didn't know much about baking.

Baking was a new world with a lot of new words.

"*Folding. Creaming,*" he said, scratching his head. "How d'you make cream out of sugar and butter?" Jamila stood beside him with a bowl of ice-cold butter which was refusing to have anything to do with a big pile of sugar.

"I think you have to beat them together really fast," said Jamila. "That's what Nani used to do." Jamila's Nani had been a really good baker. Jamila tried to beat as fast as Nani had done, until her hand hurt, but nothing happened. "It seems *really* hard."

It *was* really hard. So was the butter.

Jamila's dad tried. The block of butter got a bit sugary, but continued to look un-cream-like. "I know Nani was strong, but this is ridiculous," he said.

Jamila suddenly missed Nani very much. Her dad gave her a hug. Farhan did, too.

"I know, it's sad Nani's not here anymore," said Dad. "But I tell you something, Jamila – she'd be proud of you for entering this cake race."

Jamila smiled a bit, and blew her nose. She went back to the recipe. "We need four big eggs," she said. "And flour."

"We've got three normal-sized eggs,"
said Dad. He was also making pasta
sauce for supper whilst holding
Farhan on his hip, who
was hitting him on
the head with a
wooden spoon.
"They'll do.
And I've
got some
flour here."
He was
wearing
an apron which said, 'World's Greatest
Cook EVER'. Both he and the apron
were starting to look a little frayed
around the edges.

An hour later, the cake was out.

It had been quite hard
to get it out of the tin.

"It's flat,"
said Jamila.
"And grey."

"Grey cake,"
agreed Farhan, nodding seriously.

It didn't look like it was going to win.

"Don't worry, Jamila," said Mum,
who'd just arrived home. "Let's have
another go at the weekend – I'll help
you. We'll use the right number of eggs.
And the *right* sort of flour..."

Jamila's dad made a *Pshaw*-sounding
noise and served up his delicious pasta.

Jamila and Mum made another cake on Saturday. It wasn't grey, or flat.

But it wasn't like the cakes Nani used to make. It was dry. It was crumbly. And it tasted of…

"…nothing," said Jamila glumly. "How am I going to make a cake that tastes of joyful Jamila? How am I going to make a cake that wins?"

CHAPTER FOUR

The Great Cake Race was only one week away. Jamila still didn't know what cake she was going to make. And her cakes still tasted of cardboard.

"Cheer up and help me with these boxes," said Jamila's dad, staggering in from the garage.

"Boxes aren't going to help me," said Jamila, glumly.

"You never know," said her dad.
"In fact – if you look in this one, I think
you might find just what you need."
He gave her a wink.

Jamila sat on the floor and opened the
box. It was full to the brim with books.

Nani's baking books.

The pages were splattered with cake mix, and scattered with Nani's elegant handwriting. Jamila found herself full of memories and smiles.

Ginger cake with orange and spice – the cake Nani had always had ready for Jamila after school.

Lemon drizzle cake, sticky with syrup – Nani's favourite.

Chocolate cake with chocolate buttons on top – Jamila's special birthday cake.

Banana and walnut cake – topped with Nani's famous cream cheese icing.

It was like remembering Nani all over again. As if Jamila was next to her, watching her stirring bowls of cake mix.

But best of all were Nani's notes and tips.

Take butter and eggs out of the fridge a few hours in advance for easy creaming and beating!

Sieve the flour first (MAKE SURE IT'S THE RIGHT FLOUR!).

Taste as you go.

A spoonful of honey is like a spoonful of love.

Folding is gentle and slow.
Keep in the air.
Keep in the love.

You can't bake when you're angry.
Bake and smile, my joyful Jamila!

Jamila curled up in a chair. She read and dreamt all afternoon.

"I know what I want my cake to be like," she announced.

"*Orange* for sunshine, *honey* for love, *ginger* for memories, *raisins* for Farhan, *chocolate buttons* because they're my favourite and *cream cheese icing* because it reminds me of Nani."

"It'll be my Joyful Jamila Cake!"

"That sounds truly joyful. Let's try it!" Jamila's mum said. So Jamila set to work, using Nani's notes to help.

She mixed dark brown sugar with softened butter.

She added eggs and orange zest.

She sieved the flour and mixed it with ginger.

Finally, she added dollops of honey.

Twenty minutes later, Jamila's mum took two tins of fluffy, brown sponge out of the oven.

"They smell amazing," said Mum.

" 'MAZING!" said Farhan.

Jamila sandwiched the sponges together with Nani's famous cream cheese icing and sprinkled over chocolate buttons and raisins.

"It looks spectacular," said Dad.

" 'TAC-ULAR!" said Farhan.

And it tasted even better. It tasted of happiness and memories.

"You've done it, Jamila!" said Dad. "Can I have another slice?"

" 'NOTHER SLICE!" said Farhan, holding out his plate.

Jamila felt happiness trickle through her, like the honey in the cake. "Me, too!" she grinned.

"And you know who would have

loved it?" said her mum. "Nani."

"Now," she added, "you just have to learn to bake it QUICKLY!"

*

For the next few days, Jamila did nothing but bake her cake over and over again. Mum or Dad helped with getting the hot tins in and out of the oven, but otherwise it was all Jamila. She got super quick at creaming and super gentle at folding.

Then she thought about racing her cake.

She tried four layers.

Three.

She settled on two.

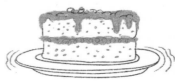

"Good job it's a tasty cake," said Dad.

*

The day before the race, Jamila and her dad went to the park to check where the race was going to be. The racetrack took them round the park, through some trees, through the playground and between two flowerbeds. It ended up in a big square of grass by the gates.

"You ready?" asked Freddie, who was doing the same.

"Yes," replied Jamila. "What about you?"

"Nearly there – just need to perfect the icing!" said Freddie. "The top layer keeps skidding off!"

"Don't worry," came Jasper's voice. "We all know I'm going to win again, so it doesn't really matter, does it?"

Jamila felt anger rising up inside her.

"Don't let him win before you start, Jamila," whispered Dad. "Remember what Nani said: *'Bake and smile!'*"

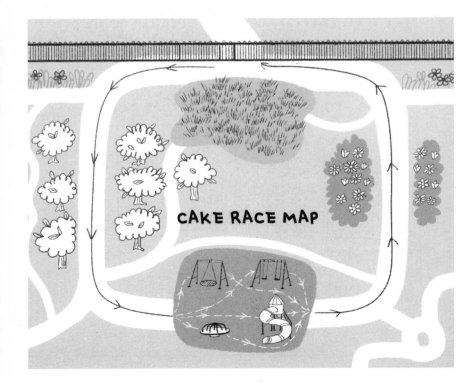

CHAPTER FIVE

The morning of the Great Cake Race
was sunny and fine.

"Perfect cake racing weather!"
said Dad, as the family walked
round to the Community Centre.
Inside, the organisers had set up
four electric cookers, each with a
table next to it. Freddie and Lulu
were already there, giving Jamila
welcoming grins.

"I'm Emma," said a woman with a big JUDGE label. "Welcome! It's such an exciting day!"

"And I'm Martin," said a man with another JUDGE label. "Good luck, everybody."

"And I'm Bernard Bun!" said Bernard Bun, coming in through the door, wearing a big apron which said **BAKE ME A CAKE!** Suddenly the atmosphere in the room, which was already at Excitement Level 10, seemed to shoot up way past 100, with added fireworks.

"So pleased to meet you!" said Lulu, shaking Bernard's hand so hard her bracelets rattled.

"You're our youngest contestant yet," Bernard Bun said to Jamila, with a warm smile. "Bake well!"

The judges explained the rules. The baking would start at 10 am. The judges would supervise the baking and taste the cakes at the end of the race.

"For Jamila and Freddie," Emma explained, "we'll take your cakes in and out of the oven for you."

The cakes had to be baked and iced by 11.30 am. If they weren't ready, they couldn't be raced. Then the race in the park would begin!

"Good luck, Jamila!" said Mum. "We'll see you at the start!" Just then Jasper strode in, with the smug air of a champion boxer.

"I'm surprised he's not wearing a cape," muttered Freddie.

"SO nice of you to come," Jasper smirked at Jamila, as he set up his equipment, including his trophies.

"We do need a contest – even if the winner is beyond doubt," he added.

Bake and smile, Jamila reminded herself. "May the fastest baker win!" she smiled.

The clock inched forwards to 10 am.

"Everyone ready?" said Emma. "The Great Cake Race starts... NOW!"

Jamila measured... and creamed.

She sieved... and stirred.

She added the ginger, honey and orange zest.

She tasted, she added a little more – and glanced around at how everyone else was doing.

Freddie was stirring vigorously, with Martin looking on. Lulu was picking out bits of eggshell, watched by an anxious Emma.

But Jasper – Jasper seemed to be ready already!

"Wow – that's amazing!" said Jamila. "I can see why you've won so many times."

"I know," smirked Jasper. He raised his bowl to her. The bowl had some paper stuck to the bottom.

"Er – I think your recipe's stuck?" said Jamila, pointing.

"My… what?" Jasper suddenly seemed flustered. "What do you mean?"

"This," said Jamila, gently. She picked off the paper.

It seemed to be a packet. It said **CAKE MIX** on it.

Jamila gasped. "You're using a ready-made cake mix, Jasper! You're… *cheating!*"

"What's that?" said Martin, coming over.

"The little girl's confused," blustered Jasper, screwing up the paper and throwing it away before Martin could see. "Doesn't know what she's saying. Running behind, too, so I'm helping her

– out of the kindness of my heart."

"But–" Jamila looked at the clock in desperation. She had to get her cake in the oven.

"That's nice, Jasper," said Martin, beaming. "So good of you to help our youngest contestant." Jamila felt anger rising in her like bubbles in a glass of lemonade.

With a furious glance, Jasper slammed his cake in the oven so fast that mixture slopped out and splattered on the floor.

'You can't bake when you're angry, Jamila.' Jamila heard Nani's voice in her head.

You're not going to ruin my cake, Jasper, Jamila thought.

She took a breath, and gave Jasper a big smile.

Carefully, gently, Jamila folded the mixture.

Carefully, gently, she scraped it into the tins.

"They look wonderful," said Emma, putting Jamila and Freddie's cakes in the oven.

"Whew!" grinned Jamila, wiping her forehead, as the clock ticked onwards.

All the cakes were now in the ovens,
and the contestants moved on to icing.

Once the cakes were out,
the challenge was to get them cool
enough to ice as quickly as possible.
Everyone had different methods.

There was
one minute to go
as Jamila put the
finishing touches to a flower made of
raisins and chocolate buttons.

"Ready, everyone?!" called Bernard Bun.

"Nearly!" cried Jamila.

Five seconds to go. Four, three, two, one...

Jamila arranged the last raisin. "DONE!"

"Fabulous job, everyone!" said Bernard Bun. All the cakes were ready to race.

Jasper glared at Jamila. "You tell anyone," he muttered, "and I'll tell them you were the one cheating!"

Jamila simply gave him a big grin.

Bake and smile, she reminded herself.
No – <u>race</u> and smile.

Together, the bakers and judges
walked through cheering crowds to the
park and the start line.
Jamila saw her mum,
dad and Farhan.

"Go, Jamila!
We'll see
you on the
finish line!"

"Ready everyone?" said Emma.
"Right! The RACE starts... NOW!"

CHAPTER SIX

Jamila started to run.

"Please don't slip," she whispered,
to herself and the cake.

The cake, anchored to the plate
with Nani's famous cream cheese icing,
happily stayed put, whilst Jamila ran like
the wind from the park gates and down
the big avenue of trees.

Beside her, Freddie was trotting
rather than running, trying to keep
his cake in place. They rounded a

corner and some of his cake tried to head in the other direction.

"WOOOAH there!" gasped Freddie, grasping the top two layers.

"Good catch, Freddie!" puffed Lulu. "Don't let it get awaaaaay!" Her cake wobbled on its plate as they headed out of the avenue towards the playground.

Jamila just managed to avoid Jasper, who pushed past.

"Take no notice, pet," panted Lulu.

"He's just too keen to win. You're doing BRILLIANTLY!"

The race got a bit complicated in the playground. There were some sticky moments as they tried to figure out the exact route they had to take.

"Wheeee!" yelled Jamila on the swings.

"Watch out!" said Freddie on the slide.

"Easy!" sniffed Jasper on the roundabout.

"Noooooo!" said Lulu in the basket swing. It was all a bit much for her cake, which leapt in the air, did a spectacular spin... and tumbled out of the net.

"Bad luck, Lulu!" said Jamila.

"Don't worry," said Lulu, picking up bits of cake. "It's still edible, that's the important thing! You go, pet!"

Jamila and Freddie ducked out of the playground gate, narrowly avoiding Jasper, and ran onto a gravel path through the middle of two flower beds.

The path was quite narrow – just wide enough for two people to run alongside each other.

Definitely not wide enough for three.

"Oi, watch it!" said Freddie, as Jasper pushed between the two of them.

Jamila's cake wobbled but stayed put. Jamila's insides wobbled, too, but she wasn't going to let that stop her.

It was too much, however, for Freddie's four layers. The top two layers, slick with icing, pirouetted off

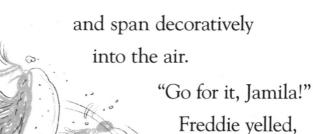

and span decoratively
into the air.

"Go for it, Jamila!"
Freddie yelled,
as he fell,
clutching
the rest of
his cake.

"Ha! Just you and me left," sniffed
Jasper, as he sped up, matched by Jamila
at every step.

"Nearly there!" panted Jamila. She
could see her family, the judges and
Bernard Bun at the finish line.

"Nearly there... Nearly –"

And then she staggered, as Jasper

shoved past her for the final time. "No one's going to win this race apart from me!"

Jamila found herself jigging like a clockwork toy to stay upright. The crowd gasped in dismay, making Jasper look round – and then, just as Jamila regained her balance, Jasper lost his!

He rocked, he spun, he twisted... and fell down, face first...

...**SPLAT!** in his own cake.

"JAMILAJAMILAJAMILAAAA!"
Farhan's voice reached Jamila above
the crowd.

The finish line was gleaming. *'Race
and smile!'* said Nani's voice.

Jamila ran like she'd never run before.

She crossed the finish line,
holding her joyful cake in the air.

She found herself in a sea of hugs,
many of them quite sticky. Especially
from Lulu and Freddie, who had
joined them.

"You did it!"

"Hooray!"

"Congratulations, Jamila," said
Bernard Bun.

"But first we need to taste it…"

Jamila held her breath
as Bernard Bun
tried a slice
of her cake.

"OOOH!"
he breathed.
"It tastes
fabulous.
It tastes of sun.
And care. Well
done, Jamila! You're a worthy winner!"
He presented her with the trophy.

Jasper tried to creep away unseen,
but as he was covered in his own slimy
cake, this wasn't easy.

"As for you, Jasper Dedicoat," Emma said, so loudly that everyone could hear, "you will never be able to enter the Great Cake Race again, you cheat! We found the cake mix wrapper!"

"That's one unbroken record that's well and truly broken," Freddie said, as Jasper walked sheepishly away, leaving big dollops of undercooked cake behind him.

Jamila smiled. She felt a bit sorry for Jasper – but not *too* sorry.

"And now… for the best bit," said Dad, taking the cake from Bernard Bun and giving it to Jamila.

"BESTBITBESTBIT!" said Farhan.

"Come on, Jamila!" said Mum.
"I can't wait any longer!"

Jamila held her cake in the air,
grinning.

"Anyone want a slice of cake?"

READING ZONE!

QUIZ TIME

Can you remember the answers
to these questions?

· Who wins the contest every year?

· What does Jamila's dad find so tricky
about baking rather than cooking?

· Why does Jamila choose to bake
two layers of cake instead of four?

· Which piece of playground equipment
is Lulu on when her cake falls?

READING ZONE!

WHAT DO YOU THINK?

Jasper reminds everyone that he has won every year and that he believes he will win again.

Why is Jasper so sure he will win?

Do you think it is right to 'win' by cheating like he does? How do you think it would feel to 'win' something when you have not followed the rules?

READING ZONE!

STORYTELLING TOOLKIT

Nani becomes one of the most important characters, even though she is no longer alive.

How does the author introduce Nani to the reader?

How is Jamila helped by Nani?

Do you ever think of someone you no longer see and remember things you learned from them?

READING ZONE!

GET CREATIVE

Jamila designs her own cake and calls it her 'Joyful Jamila Cake'.

If you could bake your own cake, what would you put in it? What decorations would it have?

How many layers would it have if you were going to race it?

You could try drawing your cake and labelling it.

Radiation Protection

1 Week Loan

This book is due for return on or before the last date shown below

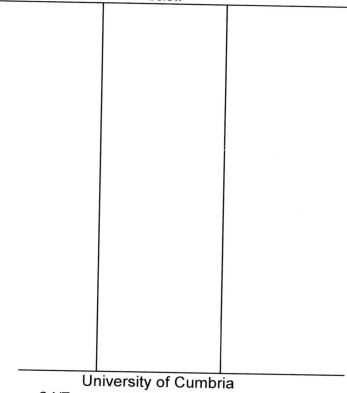

University of Cumbria
24/7 renewals Tel:0845 602 6124

NUCLEAR ENERGY AGENCY
ORGANISATION FOR ECONOMIC CO-OPERATION AND DEVELOPMENT

ORGANISATION FOR ECONOMIC CO-OPERATION AND DEVELOPMENT

Pursuant to Article 1 of the Convention signed in Paris on 14th December 1960, and which came into force on 30th September 1961, the Organisation for Economic Co-operation and Development (OECD) shall promote policies designed:

- to achieve the highest sustainable economic growth and employment and a rising standard of living in Member countries, while maintaining financial stability, and thus to contribute to the development of the world economy;
- to contribute to sound economic expansion in Member as well as non-member countries in the process of economic development; and
- to contribute to the expansion of world trade on a multilateral, non-discriminatory basis in accordance with international obligations.

The original Member countries of the OECD are Austria, Belgium, Canada, Denmark, France, Germany, Greece, Iceland, Ireland, Italy, Luxembourg, the Netherlands, Norway, Portugal, Spain, Sweden, Switzerland, Turkey, the United Kingdom and the United States. The following countries became Members subsequently through accession at the dates indicated hereafter: Japan (28th April 1964), Finland (28th January 1969), Australia (7th June 1971), New Zealand (29th May 1973), Mexico (18th May 1994), the Czech Republic (21st December 1995), Hungary (7th May 1996), Poland (22nd November 1996) and the Republic of Korea (12th December 1996). The Commission of the European Communities takes part in the work of the OECD (Article 13 of the OECD Convention).

NUCLEAR ENERGY AGENCY

The OECD Nuclear Energy Agency (NEA) was established on 1st February 1958 under the name of the OEEC European Nuclear Energy Agency. It received its present designation on 20th April 1972, when Japan became its first non-European full Member. NEA membership today consists of 27 OECD Member countries: Australia, Austria, Belgium, Canada, Czech Republic, Denmark, Finland, France, Germany, Greece, Hungary, Iceland, Ireland, Italy, Japan, Luxembourg, Mexico, the Netherlands, Norway, Portugal, Republic of Korea, Spain, Sweden, Switzerland, Turkey, the United Kingdom and the United States. The Commission of the European Communities also takes part in the work of the Agency.

The mission of the NEA is:

- to assist its Member countries in maintaining and further developing, through international co-operation, the scientific, technological and legal bases required for a safe, environmentally friendly and economical use of nuclear energy for peaceful purposes, as well as
- to provide authoritative assessments and to forge common understandings on key issues, as input to government decisions on nuclear energy policy and to broader OECD policy analyses in areas such as energy and sustainable development.

Specific areas of competence of the NEA include safety and regulation of nuclear activities, radioactive waste management, radiological protection, nuclear science, economic and technical analyses of the nuclear fuel cycle, nuclear law and liability, and public information. The NEA Data Bank provides nuclear data and computer program services for participating countries.

In these and related tasks, the NEA works in close collaboration with the International Atomic Energy Agency in Vienna, with which it has a Co-operation Agreement, as well as with other international organisations in the nuclear field.